One day he ran away. He ran until
he came to the great marsh where
the wild ducks lived. The duckling
was very tired.

He lay in the rushes for two whole
days. Then the wild ducks and some

geese came to look at him. "You're very ugly," they said, and they laughed at him.

The poor ugly duckling ran away
from the great marsh. He ran and
ran over the fields and meadows.

The wind blew and the duckling was cold and tired.

It was getting dark. The duckling
found a little cottage. It was very
old and the door was falling off.
This left a gap just big enough for
the duckling to creep inside out of
the cold.

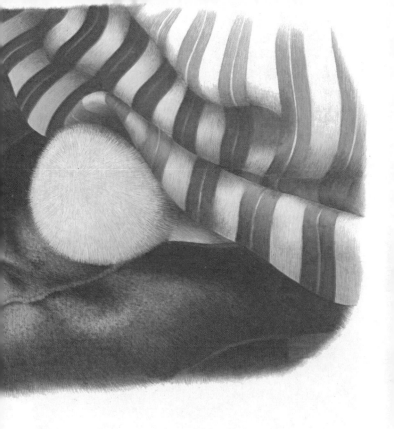

An old woman lived in the cottage.
She had a cat which could purr and
a hen which laid eggs. They found
the ugly duckling in the morning.

The old woman said, "You can stay.

Now we shall have duck eggs."

So the duckling stayed but he did
not lay eggs.

The cat said to him, "Can you purr?"

"No," said the duckling.

The hen said, "Can you lay eggs?"

"No," said the duckling, sadly.

"Then you must go," said the cat and the hen.

The ugly duckling went away again.

He walked in the marshes and

floated on the water. Everywhere he

went, birds and animals said, " How
big and ugly you are."

Winter was coming. The leaves had
dropped from the trees. The ground

was cold and hard and the duckling

had nowhere to stay.

One evening a flock of birds flew overhead. They were beautiful white swans with long necks.

"I wish I was like that," said the duckling.

The winter grew colder. The duckling had to peck at the ice to find water. One night, he was so tired he fell asleep on the ice.

In the morning a farmer found the duckling.

He took him home for his wife to
look after.

When the duckling was better, the farmer's children wanted to play with him. He was frightened and tried to run away from them.

He flew into the milk churn and
then landed in a barrel of flour. The
children laughed and tried to catch
him. The duckling ran far away.

He hid among reeds in the marsh all through the long, cold winter.

Then the warm spring sun came. The duckling spread his wings. They were strong wings now and he flew high into the air.

He flew over the canal and saw three
beautiful swans. As he landed, the
duckling saw himself in the water.
He was not an ugly duckling at all.
He was a beautiful white swan!

"Come with us," said the other
swans.

And he did.